ROSEMARY WEI

MAX'S
CHRISTMAS

PUFFIN BOOKS

For Beexoo Wells

PUFFIN BOOKS
Published by the Penguin Group
Penguin Putnam Books for Young Readers, 345 Hudson Street, New York, New York 10014, U.S.A.
Penguin Books Ltd, 27 Wrights Lane, London W8 5TZ, England
Penguin Books Australia Ltd, Ringwood, Victoria, Australia
Penguin Books Canada Ltd, 10 Alcorn Avenue, Toronto, Ontario, Canada M4V 3B2
Penguin Books (N.Z.) Ltd, 182-190 Wairau Road, Auckland 10, New Zealand

Penguin Books Ltd, Registered Offices: Harmondsworth, Middlesex, England

First published in the United States of America by Dial Books for Young Readers, a division of Penguin
Books USA Inc., 1986
Published by Puffin Pied Piper Books, 1994
Reissued by Puffin Books, a division of Penguin Putnam Books for Young Readers, 2000

3 5 7 9 10 8 6 4 2

THE LIBRARY OF CONGRESS HAS CATALOGED THE DIAL EDITION AS FOLLOWS:
Wells, Rosemary, Max's Christmas.
Summary: Max waits up on Christmas Eve to see Santa Claus coming down the chimney.
(1. Christmas—Fiction. 2. Santa Claus—Fiction. 3. Rabbits—Fiction.)
I. Title.
PZ7.W46843Masg 1986 [E] 85-27547
ISBN 0-8037-0289-2
ISBN 0-8037-0290-6 (lib. bdg.)

Puffin Books ISBN 0-14-056751-8

Printed in Mexico

The full-color artwork consists of black line-drawings and full-color washes. The black line is prepared and photographed separately for greater sharpness and contrast. The full-color washes are prepared with colored inks. They are then camera-separated and reproduced as red, yellow, blue, and black halftones.

"Guess what, Max!"
said Max's sister, Ruby.
"What?" said Max.

"It's Christmas Eve, Max," said Ruby,
"and you know who's coming!"
"Who?" said Max.

"Santa Claus is coming,
that's who," said Ruby.
"When?" said Max.

"Tonight, Max, he's coming tonight!"
  said Ruby.
"Where?" said Max.
"Spit, Max," said Ruby.

"Santa Claus is coming right down
our chimney into our living room,"
said Ruby.
"How?" said Max.

"That's enough questions, Max.

You have to go to sleep fast,
before Santa Claus comes," said Ruby.

But Max wanted to stay up
to see Santa Claus.
"No, Max," said Ruby.

"Nobody ever sees Santa Claus."
"Why?" said Max.
"BECAUSE!" said Ruby.

But Max didn't believe a word
Ruby said.

So he sneaked downstairs . . .

and waited for Santa Claus.

Max waited a long time.

Suddenly, ZOOM! Santa
jumped down the chimney
into the living room.

"Don't look, Max!" said Santa Claus.
"Why?" said Max.
"Because," said Santa Claus,
"nobody is supposed to see me!"

"Why?" said Max.
"Because everyone is supposed to be asleep in bed," said Santa Claus.

But Max peeked at Santa anyway.
"Guess what, Max!" said Santa Claus.
"What?" said Max.

"It's time for me to go away
and you to go to sleep,"
said Santa Claus.
"Why?" said Max.

"BECAUSE!" said Santa Claus.

Ruby came downstairs.
"What happened, Max?" asked Ruby.
"Who were you talking to?
Where did you get that hat?

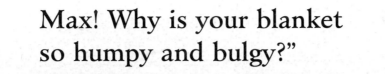

Max! Why is your blanket
so humpy and bulgy?"

"BECAUSE!" said Max.